THE BIG HOUSE

THE
WORKHOUSE BOY

A Victorian Adventure

Written and illustrated by

George Buchanan

W

FRANKLIN WATTS
LONDON•SYDNEY

THE BIG HOUSE

Winter 1858

If you leave the bustling town of Staddon and walk carefully down the track from the common, you'll see the small village of Dalcombe clustered in a steep valley. Stop and look into the distance, where the woods meet the patchwork of fields. You can just glimpse the Big House, Dalcombe Manor.

Mr Edward de Ray lives there with his granddaughter, Charlotte. Charlotte's father Jack, Mr Edward's son, comes to visit them from London from time to time.

Mrs Duff, the cook, lives there too. Her little flat overlooks the orchard. Vincent, the stableboy, occupies a small attic room and Meg and Mary, the maids, share another.

The houseboys, Albert and Fergus, have the middle room. The window is cracked. I think Fergus broke it – up to mischief as usual!

All the staff are working at the moment. It's a typical day at the Big House...

CONTENTS

CHAPTER ONE
Dirty Shoes!

'Sophia, this really won't do!'

With a sigh, Sophia de Ray put down her knife and fork. Why couldn't breakfast in the Big House ever be a peaceful occasion?

'What's the matter, Father?' she asked patiently.

'This is supposed to have been cleaned,'

complained Edward de Ray, shaking a black boot under her nose. 'Look, there's no shine on it, and,' he turned it over, 'the instep hasn't even had a lick of polish.'

Sophia tutted sympathetically. As the Master of Dalcombe Manor, Edward was used to having his own way. 'Well, Father, do remember that we're short of staff. Albert has been doing all the boots and shoes in addition to his own work, ever since you got rid of Chips six weeks ago.'

'I was quite right to get rid of him. Chips was the laziest servant we've ever employed. Dishonest, too. But that still doesn't excuse slip-shod work by Albert. I'm due at the election hustings this morning and no one is going to vote for a man with dirty boots.'

'Very well, then. The answer is simple. We need another houseboy. I shall go to the Ragged School in Staddon tomorrow and get a new boy to do the boots.'

'Can I come with you please, Aunt Sophia?'

Charlotte de Ray had been sitting at the table, eating her breakfast quietly. Her grandfather, Edward, expected children to be seen and not heard. But this was too good an opportunity to miss.

'If you behave yourself today and don't climb any trees, and if I receive a good report about you from Miss Franks,' said Sophia, 'then you may accompany me.'

Charlotte's face lit up. A whole day out of the schoolroom, away from her governess! She'd always wanted to visit the Ragged School, too. Although the de Ray family helped to fund the Staddon school for poor children, they very rarely visited it.

'And get a boy who can read and write properly,' shouted Edward as he stomped out of the room. 'Remember, I intend to be elected as Member of Parliament for Staddon, so we'll need someone who can help me in my duties.

I asked Albert to write down a list for me the other day, and I couldn't read a word of the scrawl. His writing is appalling.' The door of the breakfast room slammed shut behind him.

'I like Albert,' said Charlotte, as she reached for the bread and butter. 'He's fun. Let's choose another boy like him, Aunt Sophia.'

'We are not seeking a playmate for you, Charlotte,' said Sophia. 'You spend far too much time playing already, as can be seen from the state of your clothes. What have you done to that dress?'

Charlotte tried to hide the long rip in the skirt of her frock. 'I'm afraid I tore it yesterday and Meg was too busy to mend it.'

Aunt Sophia sniffed. 'I think I'll get a new girl from the Ragged School tomorrow, as well. Someone who can sew neatly and will help the other girls with the laundry.'

Two new playmates! Charlotte wanted to clap her hands, but she kept them firmly in her lap. If she seemed too eager, her aunt might decide not to take her to Staddon after all.

Sophia rose from her chair. 'It's time you were at your lessons. And I expect you to be on your best behaviour at the Ragged School tomorrow. Remember, we are looking for good and faithful servants who will be a credit to Dalcombe Manor. Children who will be truly grateful for an opportunity to change their lives.'

CHAPTER TWO
A New Treasure

Unaware that his life was about to change, Fergus Donovan clung to the chimney of a house overlooking the main street of Staddon.

It was an uncomfortable perch, but it gave a good view of the shabby wooden stage which was the election hustings. He should have been at school, but Mr Harris, the headteacher, had sent him out on an errand, so he thought he'd take his time and look at the election preparations. It was really interesting. Colourful flags and banners were draped around the stage. Eight men in coats and top hats huddled together on the platform, talking and nervously eyeing the jostling crowd. Another two men, accompanied by boos and cheers, sidled out and joined the committee on the platform.

A cabbage landed with a thump on the planks and rolled off the stage. Eager hands grabbed at it. It would make good ammunition. Fergus wriggled into a more comfortable position on the tiles.

On a signal from the stage, a band struck up 'Hearts of Oak' and the shouting changed to a chant.

'Hurray, hurray, de Ray!'

People waved hats and ribbons in the air and continued to chant.

'Hurray, hurray, de Ray!'

Then, above the hubbub, Fergus heard his name called.

'Fergus Donovan! Come down here, you little rat!'

Fergus looked down and his heart froze as he recognised the two men who were waving at him. Silas Nicks and his crony, Chips! Nicks helped out at Mill Street Refuge – the refuge where Fergus slept every night. He was bad

news. And his new friend, Chips, who had only moved in a month ago, was almost as bad.

Fergus leaned over the parapet. 'What do you want?' he called.

'Get down here, or I'll come up and get you myself!'

Fergus swallowed hard. He leaned out, grabbed the lamppost and slid down to the pavement.

'What can I do for you, Mr Nicks, Sir?' he asked, trembling.

Nicks towered over him. 'Get in that crowd and nick us some hankies.'

'Pretty ones,' growled Chips. 'Worth sixpence or better.'

'Can't do that,' said Fergus and put his hand up to shield the blow he knew was coming, 'it ain't right to steal.'

'You wouldn't want us to hurt you now, would you?' threatened Nicks. 'Or that stupid old friend of yours, Jacky?'

Fergus trembled. His only friend in the refuge was old Jacky. Years ago he had been a famous fighter, before all the hard punches had made him slow and shaky. But he was kind and gentle, and when Fergus was first thrust into the frightening world of the refuge, Jacky had watched out for him.

'Get on with it, or Jacky gets his face kicked in tonight!' yelled Nicks, giving Fergus a shove which sent him reeling into the crowd.

'I ain't gonna do it,' Fergus muttered to himself as he pushed and squeezed his way through the throng. An image of old Jacky flashed into his mind and he shivered. Would Nicks dare carry out his threat?

The crowd surged forward. Looking up, Fergus saw a tall man wearing a white top hat and coat step to the edge of the platform and signal for quiet. He was carrying a cane with a shiny top, which he waved above his head. The roar from the crowd grew louder. The band reached a deafening crescendo and stopped.

'Good people,' the man began, but his voice was drowned out by the mob.

'None of 'em here, mate!' someone shouted.

'Get off, de Ray!'

'We want Smith! Smith for Staddon!'

'I beg you,' the tall man tried again, but the hecklers gave him no chance. There was more laughter and catcalls. One man started making rude noises, blowing across the back of his hand.

'Smith, Smith, Smith for Staddon!'

'Good people, a brief word.' The tall man tried for a third time to make himself heard. The crowd's roar had reached a deafening level and people started to throw things. Fruit, vegetables, eggs and clumps of turf began raining on to the stage.

A cabbage hit the tall man hard in the face. He staggered backwards before falling and banging his head on the platform. His cane sailed into the air. Fergus watched. It was coming straight at him. Hands shot up. Men leapt to catch it and jostled for possession, but the cane slipped through their fingers and fell,  with a clatter, on to the cobbles at Fergus's feet.

He dived, grabbed the cane quickly, slipped it under his frayed coat and darted away. Hands snatched and grabbed at him, but Fergus slid like an eel through the jungle of swaying and kicking legs, struggling towards the edge of the crowd.

Glancing behind him, he saw the tall man being carried off the platform, blood pouring from his head. Fergus dashed away clutching his coat tightly about him.

'Must get it safe,' he muttered to himself as he ran headlong round the corner into Mansion Street. Darting in front of a horse-cab, he slipped through some iron railings and into the laurel bushes of a deserted house. In their secret shadows, he stole to the wall of the house where an iron grate was fixed to the stones. He lifted it quietly, checked no one was watching, put both feet together and slid down a black chute into an underground vault.

Fergus waited a moment until his eyes adjusted to the darkness. Then, he pulled the stick from his coat and slid his fingers along the polished shaft of the cane. At the top there was a carved knob – it felt cold and smooth. With extreme care, he held it up to the murky light and gazed at it in wonder. It was meant to be some sort of animal. It looked like a mouse with pointed ears and a long, fluffy tail. He was sure he'd seen something like it before but couldn't remember where. As Fergus pondered, he rubbed the little creature against the sleeve of his shirt and it shone with a deep, yellow glow.

'This is a beautiful thing,' he whispered to himself. 'It might be valuable. I must hide it carefully and try to give it back to the owner.'

Carefully, he picked his way across the floor, reached up and pulled a bundle of sacking from the disused fireplace. He opened the bundle and looked at his treasures – a little dented pewter mug, a small wooden ring  from a hoopla stall, a knife with a rusty blade and the brass end of a telescope. Reverently, he added the stick to his precious collection, wrapped them up again and slid the bundle back into the chimney.

'It must be getting dark,' he muttered, as he started to scramble back into the street. 'Jacky will be waiting for me at the refuge. I won't be able to get in if I'm late.'

CHAPTER THREE
The Mill Street Refuge

Fergus made it just in time. The doors of the men's refuge were still open, throwing a yellow light onto the black cobbles. A file of men and boys shuffled through the doors. Fergus tagged onto the end of the line and as he stepped into the smoky, crowded warmth of the workhouse, the doors clanged behind him. He looked around anxiously for Jacky and soon spotted him towering above the men huddled round the stove.

Fergus breathed a sigh of relief. He dodged through the crowd and pulled at Jacky's coat. The old man looked down and beamed with pleasure.

'Jacky,' Fergus whispered. 'I've got a new treasure!' Jacky put out his huge hand and ruffled Fergus's hair. His watery eyes twinkled with a smile.

'It's a walking stick!' said Fergus.

'A stick?' laughed Jacky. 'And what will you be doing with a stick at your age?'

'It's a beautiful stick, Jacky. I've put it with my other treasures.'

'Hands and faces! Hands and faces!' bawled a voice, interrupting them.

It was the signal for them all to wash. Fergus and Jacky stood in line, waiting their turn. Just as Jacky reached a sink, Silas Nicks jumped out behind him.

'Clean that muck off, Jacky!' he shouted, raised his foot and kicked the old man in the back, sending him flying against the sink.

'Stop it!' screamed Fergus.

'Old fool,' muttered Nicks, turning away from Jacky and grabbing Fergus by the shoulders. 'Head right in,' he shouted and kicked him behind the knees. Fergus's knees

buckled and he hit his front tooth on the edge
of the sink. Nicks pulled at his ear.

'Where's the cane?' he hissed.

'I ain't got no cane.'

'Chips saw you with it, you workhouse
scum! Don't lie!'

'I ain't got it!' cried Fergus angrily.

'Liar!' hissed Nicks, moving back to Jacky,
who was holding tightly to the sink and
breathing in great gasps of air.

'Come on,
man!' he shouted.
'Don't stand
there dribbling.
Wash yourself!'
He turned again
to Fergus. 'And,
I'll fix *you* later!'

Fergus
limped away,
looking for
somewhere to
sleep. The beds
by the stove
were taken by

Nicks's pals. Fergus chose a bed in the corner and sat on the rolled-up blanket. Jacky lowered himself stiffly onto the next cot. There was very little noise. Just the sound of Nicks and his pals laughing by the stove and the coughing and sneezing of the weak.

Suddenly, the doors of the refuge swung open and three men entered. Two of them carried large wicker baskets. The sweet smell of fresh bread filled the hall.

'How many paupers tonight, Mr Nicks?' a voice called.

'A full house again, Mr Robinson,' shouted Nicks.

'Rubbish,' murmured Fergus to Jacky. 'There's a row of empty beds against the wall. I bet he's going to sell the leftovers.'

Chips and another man took the baskets and began to distribute the little loaves.

Mr Robinson began reciting the evening prayers. Gradually the beggars and urchins joined in and the hall filled with the low hum of 'amen' and 'thank you kindly', as each took his small loaf.

Mr Robinson finished. 'Goodnight to you

all and may tomorrow bring you a better day,' he said kindly and turned to go, ushering his two assistants in front of him.

'Lights out, Mr Nicks,' he called, locking the door behind him. One by one the gas jets were turned down until only the red glow of the stove brightened the room. Everybody soon fell asleep and the room resounded with snores and wheezy rattles.

In the gloom Fergus lay unable to sleep. Suddenly, he noticed two shadowy figures moving amongst the sleeping bodies. With a heavy heart he recognised Nicks and Chips.

They must be looking for him! Where could he hide? Perhaps if he snuggled up to Jacky and lay very still?

Fergus crawled quietly across the edge of his cot and slid in next to Jacky. He wriggled under the blanket. Didn't old Jacky smell! Gingerly, Fergus moved the blanket to cover them both.

Just in time!

'I thought he was about here,' whispered Chips.

'Yeah, I saw him next to Jacky.'

'Coo, it stinks round here! Where is the little rat?'

Fergus lay with his face pressed into the dirty blanket. Every time he breathed he inhaled a gritty dust. He was going to choke! He rammed his sleeve into his mouth and shook in silent convulsions.

'He's here!'

A pair of strong hands dragged him from the cot.

'Bring him to the stove!' said Nicks.

Fergus was hauled across the room and dumped near the stove.

'Where's the cane, Fergus?' Nicks whispered. 'Chips says it's valuable.'

'S'right,' growled Chips. 'I worked for that stinker Edward de Ray for six weeks and he never went anywhere without that stick. Solid gold the head was. Worth a fortune.'

'I ain't got it,' Fergus muttered.

'He's got it somewhere. I know it!'

'Where's the stick, Fergus? Where have you put it?' Nicks reached out and began to twist Fergus's arm. Fergus struggled, gasping with the pain. Then, out of the corner of his eye, he noticed a dark shadow rising from the shadows. Fergus turned away and stared at Nicks.

'It ain't yours,' he muttered and spat straight in his eye.

Nicks bellowed and yanked Fergus's arm.

Chips shouted, 'Watch out, Nicks!' But it was too late. A huge, shaggy figure staggered across the floor of the room. It was Jacky!

With a roar, he seized Chips by the neck and flung him to the ground. There was a nasty clang as Chips's head hit the metal stove. Then he turned and lashed out at Nicks. His powerful blow to Nicks's jaw knocked the slimy thief off his feet.

A crowd of people had gathered round and a cheer rose.

'Get 'em, Jacky boy!'

'Jacky Derby, you settle 'em good 'n' proper!'

'You show 'em!'

The old fighter stood swaying amongst the fallen bodies. He gasped and struggled for breath. Fergus rushed to hold him up, and together they stumbled back to their cots.

'Thanks, Jacky,' whispered Fergus. 'Are you all right?'

'Never felt happier!' he wheezed. 'It'll take more than them to stop old Jacky Derby. Bullies and cowards the lot of 'em! Don't worry about me, Ferg. It's yourself you've got to watch out for. Those two have got it in for you and this ain't a safe place anymore. You'd best think of moving on.'

Then he turned over and started to snore, leaving Fergus to his thoughts. Jacky was right. Nicks would give him no peace until he'd got the cane.

But he wasn't going to give it to him!

It belonged to the tall man who'd been hurt. Somehow he had to find a way of giving it back to him. And, in the meantime, he'd just have to find somewhere else to sleep!

CHAPTER FOUR
A Stroke of Luck

Fergus didn't sleep at all that night. He tossed and turned in his cot, puzzling about his future.

He was still worrying when the other workhouse occupants were woken by Mr Robinson. Once again loaves were distributed, but not by Chips this time. There was no sign of him or Nicks.

At six o'clock the doors opened, and a procession of paupers shuffled out into the winter darkness. Many of them had nowhere to go until the doors of the refuge were opened again in the evening.

Fergus was one of the lucky ones. He was off to school. He said goodbye to Jacky and ran off down the alley, clutching his loaf.

He had been going to the Ragged School since he was six – a whole year! He had learnt to read and count and he knew how to weigh and measure things.

Now he was learning how to make and clean boots and Mr Harris, the school manager, had asked him to join the Shoe Black Brigade. He would be able to earn at least a shilling a day as a shoe-shine boy!

The school was at the end of Water Lane. It was a large, clean, white-washed building with Water Lane Union School painted on the wall. As Fergus got closer, he saw a big blue and red cart standing outside. In front of it was a grand carriage with a big coat-of-arms on the door.

Fergus slipped into his classroom just in time. One minute later, Mr Harris entered. He was followed by a tall, thin lady wearing an eyeglass. A pretty little girl with a cheeky smile held her hand.

'Stand up, Boot Black Brigade,' snapped Mr Harris.

Fergus leapt to his feet. So did half a dozen other boys.

'Out to the front.'

The boys squeezed their way past the other pupils and lined up in front of the class. Fergus was the last boy in the line. He was also the smallest.

'These are my boys, Miss de Ray.' Mr Harris wiped his perspiring head with a hanky. 'Every one of them trained by myself. All of them can black dozens of boots a day.'

'But can they all read and write?' asked Sophia.

'Yes, Ma'm.'

Sophia de Ray marched down the line, fixing each boy in turn with a gimlet eye.

Charlotte trailed behind her, sizing them up as prospective playmates.

'You!' Sophia picked on a large boy with red hair. 'If you're paid a penny halfpenny for every pair of shoes you clean, how many pairs will you have to black to earn three shillings?'

The boy screwed up his face in thought. 'Come on! Quickly!'

The boy said nothing, but counted slowly on his fingers. The silence stretched out until Fergus could bear it no longer. 'Please, Miss,' he blurted out, 'twenty-four!'

Everyone stared at Fergus. The little girl gave him a wink.

'And what is your name?' demanded Sophia.

'Please, Ma'am, my name is Fergus Donovan.'

'Fergus Donovan,' she repeated. Her eyes swept him from head to toe. 'You're very small.'

'Yes, Miss. But I'm strong. And I'll grow.' Fergus pulled his shoulders back and rose on the points of his toes.

A smile played at the corner of Sophia's stern mouth. 'And would you like to work as a servant at Dalcombe Manor?'

Fergus had no idea where Dalcombe Manor was but anything would be better than the refuge. 'Yes please, Miss, I'd like it more than anything else in the world.'

Sophia's face softened. 'Very well then. Come with me.' And taking the little girl by the hand once again, Sophia swept out of the classroom. Fergus tagged meekly behind and followed them through the corridors and out of the front door. She paused as she entered the shiny carriage and pointed to the cart behind. 'In there. Mr Portbury will drive you to the Big House.'

Fergus clambered up the wide wooden wheel of the cart and looked down. Bundled in a corner was a girl, a few years older than himself, clutching a small bundle of clothes. He jumped down next to her.

'Hello. Who are you?' asked Fergus, smiling.

'My name's Agnes.' The girl's grip on her bundle tightened. 'And Miss de Ray picked me out this morning. I'm going to Dalcombe Manor to train to be a maid.'

'And I'm Fergus. I'm going to clean boots,' he grinned. 'Isn't it exciting?'

Agnes gave him a shy smile. 'I think this must be the luckiest day of my life,' she replied.

Fergus couldn't think of anything else to say, so he rolled over and buried his nose in the hay. The smell was wonderful! He burrowed further, enjoying the feel of the hay tickling his face and before he knew it he had dozed off.

He must have slept for some time because when he woke, the cart had left the town of Staddon behind. A windmill hung motionless in the cold air, and cows and sheep wandered freely across the icy road.

Several carts were on the road heading for market, their drivers wrapped against the cold. The children saw ducks and chickens in wicker pens, brown sacks of grain and potatoes and piles of large round turnips. A two-wheeled cart trundled slowly by, with milk churns swinging from the running board and they also passed a little girl shepherding geese along the road.

Fergus nestled back in the hay. Suddenly, he remembered his hidden treasures. Would he ever be able to return to Staddon for them?

'Is it much further, Agnes?' he asked.

Agnes leaned forward. 'How far is Dalcombe, please, Mr Portbury?' she asked.

'We're nearly there now. It's only six miles from Staddon,' the driver replied, and carried on humming to himself.

That's nothing. I can easily fetch my treasures, thought Fergus and instantly cheered up. He leaned over and tugged at Mr Portbury's sleeve. 'Please can I drive?'

'Certainly not,' said Mr Portbury, pulling up his horse in front of a pair of tall iron gates, 'but you can jump down and open these gates for me.'

Fergus leapt down and wrestled with the heavy latch. He had often earned a farthing opening gates for rich people, but these were the biggest he had opened. He looked up at the intricate ironwork, and froze momentarily. There, on the top of each gatepost, was a small animal with a big bushy tail – the same as the one on the top of his stick! Suddenly, he remembered where he had seen this animal before. It was engraved on the door of the De Ray Building Company in Staddon.

'Hurry up, lad,' called Mr Portbury.

As Fergus climbed back his face was shining with excitement. 'Mr Portbury! What are those animals on the gates?'

'Squirrels. Family emblem of the de Rays. Squirrels have always lived here, you see.'

'The man with the white hat! His stick had a squirrel on it, I saw it!' shouted Fergus excitedly. 'They hurt him. At the hustings.'

'That's right, lad. That was Miss Sophia's father, Edward de Ray, the Master of Dalcombe Manor. He was standing as a parliamentary candidate,' explained Mr Portbury. 'They carried him back unconscious yesterday, but Mrs Cater says he should soon be mended.'

'Is this his house?'

They had reached the top of the rise and below them stood a stone mansion, glowing in the morning light. It had pillars, row upon row of windows and countless chimney pots. The cart stopped at a side door.

'Yes, this is the Big House. Off you get now, and go in through the servant's entrance,' answered Mr Portbury. He handed them down and led the horse away.

Fergus and Agnes stood and gazed in awe at their new home.

'Don't stand there getting cold,' a jolly voice called out. 'Come inside into the warmth.'

CHAPTER FIVE
A Fresh Start

The maid with the welcoming voice led Fergus and Agnes through a hallway, down a stone passage and into a bright room with an iron stove, a long table and stone sinks.

Another maid was busily laying out the pots and pans for the day and a short cheerful lady, wearing a blue frock and a white apron, was carrying a steaming plate of cakes. She crossed the kitchen to greet them.

'So, you are Agnes and Fergus, come to join us! Meet Mary and Meg.' She nodded at the two maids. 'And I'm Mrs Duff, the cook. I'm not married, but I'm called Mrs Duff, anyway.' She gave a loud laugh and held out the plate. 'Help yourselves to a honeycake. You must be starving!'

Fergus tried not to eat greedily, but it was hard. He'd never tasted anything so sweet in his life. Sticky crumbs fell onto his coat and he brushed them away.

'Oh dear, Fergus, look at your clothes! They're a disgrace,' clucked Mrs Duff, plucking at the threadbare material. 'And so are you. Go along with Mary now, she'll fix you a bath and get you some new clothes. Agnes, you go with Meg.'

Mary led Fergus through a side door, across the yard and into a laundry room lined with shelves and drawers. She began searching the drawers. 'Clothes off, Fergus!' she said.

Fergus did nothing and Mary looked up. 'How can you have a bath if you won't take your clothes off?' she asked.

'No looking, then,' mumbled Fergus, and slowly pulled off his coat. He held it tightly with both hands.

Mary looked at him sympathetically. 'I'll tell you what, Fergus. I'll make you a bath next door. You leave your clothes in a pile here, wrap yourself in this towel, nip next door and wash yourself thoroughly. There will be clean clothes waiting for you. I'll make sure your old ones are washed carefully.'

She disappeared into the next room and Fergus heard the sound of pouring water.

Slowly, he pulled off his ragged shirt and peeped though the doorway. Mary had gone and under the window was a tub full of steaming water.

Fergus got in and lay in the soapy warm water. He closed his eyes and swirled his fingers, sighed happily and fell asleep. The next thing he was aware of was voices.

'He's still got his trousers on, look!'

'Look at his skin!'

'All those bruises!'

'Poor little boy!'

Fergus woke with a start. Mrs Duff, Mary and Meg were standing looking down at him.

'Fergus, you cannot bathe with your trousers on!' said Mrs Duff, firmly. With no more ado, she stripped off his trousers and scrubbed him vigorously all over. Then, she towelled him roughly dry and stood over him while he bashfully pulled on his new clothes. 'Now we'll go and see Miss Sophia.' Mrs Duff marched him along hundreds of corridors (or so it seemed to Fergus) and eventually knocked on a door.

'Come in!' called the voice of Miss Sophia.

Mrs Duff opened the door of the drawing room and pushed Fergus gently into the room. Sunlight streamed through the high windows and illuminated the bright carpets and beautiful chairs. Miss Sophia was sitting quietly by the window, reading.

She put down her eyeglasses, looked up and blinked. 'Now Fergus, you are going to learn to be a houseboy. Your first task will be to clean the boots. Albert will show you your duties. You'll be sharing a room with him. And please be aware  of the fact that my father, Mr Edward de Ray, is ill at the moment. You are to make no sound in the house. There is to be no running about! Is that understood?'

Fergus nodded. He was too nervous to speak.

'Good. You are to work hard and be a credit to the Big House. If you are idle, you will be dismissed. And remember that I will be receiving reports from Mrs Cater about your work, so no slacking!'

CHAPTER SIX
Hard Work

Fergus had never worked so hard in his life but he'd never enjoyed himself so much either. Every morning when he woke up in his new, comfortable bed, he gave thanks that he wasn't back in the refuge.

Life in the Big House was so interesting. There was something new to learn every day –

like helping Agnes hang out the washing in
the garden.

'Why do they want to hang the clothes out of
doors, Agnes?'

'So they dry quicker and so that they smell
nice and fresh when they are brought in.'

'They wouldn't smell very nice if you hung
them in Staddon.'

'Especially not if they were near the glue
factory! And they would come in covered in soot.'

They both giggled. 'Do you know we've
already been here five weeks, Agnes?'

'I know. We're both so lucky, Fergus. You with
Albert as a room mate, and me with Mary and

Meg. Even Miss Sophia is all right when you're used to her ways.'

'Who do you think wears these?' he asked, fishing out a pair of long white woolly trousers from the basket on the grass.

'I think they're Mr Edward's,' mumbled Agnes, with her mouth full of pegs. 'Though I haven't seen him since I got here. He's ill in bed.'

'I haven't seen him either. I haven't even been allowed in to his room. I leave the coals outside and...' Fergus broke off. 'Hey, look at Albert running.'

Albert was puffing so much it was a few minutes before they could make out what he was saying. 'There's a man wants to see you, Fergus. He's round the back of the coachhouse. He wants to speak to you now.'

'Me?'

'Yes, and he's an ugly-looking chap too. He caught me by the wrist and wouldn't let go until I promised to tell you.' Albert's round face looked troubled. 'I'd run there quick if I were you.'

Fergus had a sinking feeling in his stomach. He thought he knew who it was.

And he was right! At the back of the

coachhouse lurked Silas Nicks. He sidled over to Fergus with an oily smile. 'Here, Ferg lad. Nice to see you again. Like to earn yourself some money?'

Fergus hung back. He'd never seen Nicks smile before and he didn't like it.

'Like to earn yourself ten pounds?' asked Nicks again.

'Ten pounds?' Fergus's voice came out as a squeak. That was more money than he could ever hope of earning!

'Yeah. Remember that stick you got in Staddon? Well, I've got a friend who has taken a fancy to it.'

The stick! Fergus's jaw dropped open. He'd been so busy at Dalcombe Manor that he'd forgotten all about the cane.

'I haven't got it,' he said quickly.

'Well, you'd better get it then, double quick. Because I'll be back here this time tomorrow and, if you haven't got it, I'm going to break every bone in your rotten little body. Your old mate Jacky ain't here to look after you now.' Nicks spat on the ground and lurched away, leaving Fergus shaking.

What on earth was Fergus going to do? His shaky legs gave way and he slid to the ground. Muddled thoughts were running round and round in his head. He took a few deep breaths and tried to pull himself together. The answer was obvious. He must go into Staddon to get the stick and give it to Mr Edward. But he couldn't just leave his duties at the Big House. He'd have to ask Mrs Cater if he could go. Perhaps she wasn't as fierce as she seemed?

Reluctantly Fergus picked himself up and headed for the housekeeper's room. Outside her door, he paused. He could hear Mrs Cater's voice inside.

'He's very ill. That cruel blow he received at the election hustings has brought him low. But being robbed of his favourite stick at the same time has just done for him.'

'Well, I never.' Fergus could just about make out Mrs Duff's low voice.

'Yes,' continued Mrs Cater. 'It was given to him by his father and has been in the de Ray family for centuries. Of course, the handle's gold, but that's not the reason he's so upset. It's the sentimental value. He tosses and turns and mutters in his sleep asking for it.'

'Well, I never,' muttered Mrs Duff again.

Fergus turned away. How could he tell Mr Edward that he'd known where his stick was for the last five weeks? He'd have to go and fetch it and just hope that no one would miss him!

CHAPTER SEVEN
Lost and Found

It was gone eleven o'clock at night and the Big House was shrouded in darkness. The only light came from the kitchen where Mrs Duff pottered about, checking the preparations for tomorrow's luncheon. A muffled knock at the back door disturbed her activity. Who on earth could it be?

She opened the door a little way and peered out into the dark. A small weary figure met her gaze. 'Why Fergus!' she exclaimed, opening her arms to the small boy. 'Where have you been at this time of night? And look at your clothes!'

Fergus's best uniform was covered in soot and dust and in his arms he clutched a dusty bundle.

'I'm sorry, Mrs Duff. But I must see Mr de Ray,' he blurted out.

'No one disturbs Mr Edward at this time of night. You can't possibly go up!'

But Fergus skipped past her, ran down the corridor, burst through the door and raced up the stairs to Mr de Ray's dressing-room. With a pounding heart, he banged urgently on the door.

'What is it?' a weak voice called.

Fergus opened the door and stepped inside. Mr Edward was slumped in an armchair in the corner of the room. A large bandage was swathed around his head.

'Come along in, Mrs Cater,' he muttered, then looked round and started. 'Who are you?' he demanded, suddenly alert.

'Please Sir, I'm Fergus Donovan, the new houseboy.'

'Houseboy? Houseboy? And what do you mean, coming into my room at this time of night?' he thundered.

Fergus's voice shook. 'I've come to give you something,' he began. 'I'm very sorry. I know I shouldn't have taken it, but I never meant to keep it and I only found out today that it belonged
to you. Everything here is so different from the refuge and I tried to forget everything about my time there and I'm really sorry and...'

'What on earth are you talking about, boy?'

Fergus reached into the sacking and pulled out the stick. 'I think this is yours, Sir. I caught it at the hustings. I've been to fetch it from my special place in Staddon.'

Mr Edward grasped the stick. 'God bless my soul! Have you walked all the way to Staddon and back?'

Fergus nodded.

'Did you ask permission?'

'No, Sir. But I had to go.'

Mr de Ray stroked the squirrel on the top of his stick lovingly. 'You are a most extraordinary boy. Do you mean to say that you

have walked twelve miles through the dark to fetch me this?'

Fergus nodded again.

'Well, I'm extremely grateful to you, young man. The loss of this cane hurt me much more than the blow on the head. You've done me a big favour.' He lifted himself to his feet slowly with the aid of his stick. 'In fact I feel better than I've done for weeks. Is there anything I can do for you in return, Fergus Donovan?'

'Please don't send me away, Sir. I know I shouldn't have left my duties this evening and Miss Sophia said I'd be fired if I didn't work

hard.' Fergus wiped away a tear with the back of his hand. 'But this is where I want to stay, Sir.'

'And so you shall, young Fergus. Come over here.'

Fergus moved closer to his master and Edward put his hand on his shoulder. 'You are an honest lad and a credit to Dalcombe Manor. No one will send you away. Now, let's go down to the kitchen together. You must be starving after your long walk and I can feel my appetite coming back too.'

Together they made their way to the kitchen. Fergus walked slowly to keep pace with Mr Edward's slow steps and Mrs Duff welcomed them with surprise.

'Oh Mr Edward, Sir, you do look better. Sit yourselves down. You'll both want something hot to drink. And how about one of my honeycakes?' She bustled about the kitchen, producing steaming mugs of cocoa and cakes as if by magic.

Sitting side by side at the kitchen table, in the light of the flickering fire, man and boy looked gravely at each other. Mr de Ray raised his mug. 'Here's to you, Fergus, and your new life at Dalcombe Manor.'

Fergus blushed. Then he opened his mouth to speak but nothing happened. He tried again and his voice came out as a croak. 'I'm sorry, Sir, but I'm so pleased I can't think what to say.'

'Don't speak. Eat!' replied his master, taking a honeycake. With a happy sigh, Fergus chose the biggest, stickiest one on the plate.

And, as midnight struck, the workhouse boy and the man who had given him a new life, munched honeycakes in contented silence.

NOTES

SHOE BLACK BRIGADES

The Shoe Black Brigades were recruited from the pupils attending the ragged schools (see note overleaf).

By 1859, there were nine brigades in London. Each boy was trained to polish shoes and was provided with a uniform, brushes and polish. The boys could earn up to £17 per year.

REFUGES

Refuges provided overnight shelter for homeless people and were often funded by wealthy families. The conditions varied from refuge to refuge. Usually, an 8oz loaf of bread was given to each pauper (poor person) twice a day. Occasionally, coffee or soup was served. On the whole, the women's refuges were more comfortable.

THE HUSTINGS

In Victorian times, the hustings was the public platform from which the election candidates were announced and where voters publicly cast their votes. The candidates also made speeches from this platform during the election.

The Ballot Act of 1872 abolished the hustings, in favour of a secret ballot.

RAGGED SCHOOLS

Ragged schools were for children who could not afford to go to ordinary schools. The idea of the ragged schools began in 1818, when a man called John Pounden began teaching children in his workshops, whilst earning a living as a cobbler.

By that time, others, including Lord Shaftesbury and Thomas Guthrie, had also started their efforts to provide free education for the poor.

Eventually, in 1844, the Ragged School Union was formed and, by 1859, there were about 24,000 children being taught in day and evening classes at ragged schools. Pupils were taught reading and writing and other useful skills such as measuring and weighing.

The poorly paid staff of the ragged schools were helped by the older and more able pupils, who assisted with the teaching.

Like the refuges, the schools were mainly funded by wealthy families.